# The Wild Wood

*from*
## The Wind in the Willows

*Written by*
KENNETH GRAHAME

*Abridged and illustrated by*
INGA MOORE

TED SMART

# The Wild Wood

The Mole had long wanted to make the acquaintance of the Badger. But whenever he mentioned his wish to the Water Rat he always found himself put off. "Badger'll turn up some day," the Rat would say.

"Couldn't you ask him here – dinner or something?" said the Mole.

"He wouldn't come," replied the Rat simply. "Badger hates Society, and invitations, and dinner, and all that sort of thing."

"Well, supposing we call on *him*?" suggested the Mole.

"O, I'm sure he wouldn't like that at *all*," said the Rat. "He's so very shy. He'll be along some day."

But he never came along, and it was not till summer was over, and cold and frost kept them indoors, that the Mole found his thoughts dwelling again on the grey Badger.

And one cold still afternoon with a hard steely sky overhead, he slipped out of the warm parlour and went by himself to the Wild Wood, where Mr Badger lived.

There was nothing
to alarm him at first entry.
Twigs crackled under his feet, logs
tripped him, funguses on stumps startled him;
but that was all fun, and exciting. It led him on, to
where the light was less, and trees crouched nearer and
nearer, and holes made ugly mouths at him on either side.

Everything was very still now; and the light seemed to be
draining away like flood-water.

Then the faces began.

It was over his shoulder that he first thought he saw a face:
a little evil wedge-shaped face, looking out at him from a hole.
When he turned the thing had vanished.

He quickened his pace, telling himself cheerfully not to
begin imagining things, or there would be simply no end to it.
He passed another hole, and another; then – yes! – no! – yes!
a little narrow face, with hard eyes, had flashed up for an
instant and was gone. He braced himself and strode on. Then
suddenly, every hole, far and near, seemed to possess its face, all
fixing on him glances of malice and hatred: all hard-eyed and
evil and sharp.

If he could only get away from the holes in the banks, he
thought, there would be no more faces. He swung off the path
and plunged into the untrodden places of the wood.

Then the whistling began.

Very faint and shrill it was,
when first he heard it;
it made him hurry forward.
Then it sounded far ahead of him,
and made him want to go back.
As he halted it broke out on either side,
and passed throughout the whole length of the wood.
They were up and ready, whoever they were! And he – he was
alone, and unarmed, and far from help;
and the night was closing in.

Then the pattering began.

He thought it was only
falling leaves at first, so
slight was the sound
of it. Then as it grew
it took a rhythm,
and he knew it
for the pat-pat-
pat of little feet.
As he listened anxiously,
leaning this way and that,
it seemed to be closing in on him.
A rabbit came running towards him.
"Get out of this, you fool, get out!" the
Mole heard him mutter as he swung round
a stump and disappeared down a burrow.

The pattering increased till it sounded
like hail on the dry-leaf carpet spread
around him. The whole wood
seemed to be running now,
running hard, hunting,
chasing something
or – somebody?

In panic, he began to
run too. He ran
up against
things.

He fell
over things

and
into things.

He darted
under things and

dodged
round things.

At last he took refuge
in the dark hollow of
an old beech tree. He
was too tired to run any
further, and could only
snuggle down into the dry
leaves and hope he was safe
for the time. As he lay panting
and trembling, and listened to the
whistlings and patterings outside, he knew
that dread thing which other little dwellers in
field and hedgerow had encountered here and known
as their darkest moment – the Terror of the Wild Wood!

Meantime the Rat dozed by his fireside. His paper of half-finished verses slipped from his knee, his head fell back and his mouth opened. Then a coal slipped. The fire crackled and he woke with a start. He reached down to the floor for his verses, pored over them for a minute, and then looked round for the Mole to ask him if he knew a good rhyme for something or other.

But the Mole was not there.

He listened for a time. The house seemed very quiet.

Then he called "Moly!", got up and went out into the hall. The Mole's cap was missing from its accustomed peg. His goloshes, which always lay by the umbrella-stand, were also gone.

The Rat left the house and examined the muddy ground outside, hoping to find the Mole's tracks. There they were, sure enough. The goloshes were new, just bought for the winter, and the pimples on their soles were fresh and sharp. He could see the imprints of them in the mud, running along straight and purposeful, leading direct to the Wild Wood.

The Rat looked very grave. Then he re-entered the house, strapped a belt round his waist, shoved a brace of pistols into it, took up a stout cudgel that stood in a corner of the hall, and set off for the Wild Wood at a smart pace.

It was already getting towards dusk when he reached the first fringe of trees and plunged without hesitation into the wood, looking anxiously for any sign of his friend. Wicked little faces popped out of holes, but vanished at sight of the Rat, his pistols, and the great ugly cudgel in his grasp; and the whistling and pattering, which he had heard plainly on entry, died away, and all was still. He made his way through the length of the wood, calling cheerfully, "Moly! Where are you? It's me – Rat!"

He had hunted for an hour or more, when he heard a little answering cry. From out of the hole of an old beech tree came a feeble voice, saying, "Ratty! Is that really you?"

The Rat crept into the hollow, and there he found the Mole, exhausted and still trembling. "O Rat!" he cried, "I've been so frightened, you can't think!"

"You shouldn't really have gone and done it, Mole," said the Rat. "We river-bankers hardly ever come here by ourselves. If we have to come, we come in couples; then we're all right. Besides, there are a hundred things to know – passwords, and signs, and plants you carry in your pocket, and verses you repeat, and dodges and tricks; all simple enough when you know them, but they've got to be known if you're small, or you'll find yourself in trouble."

"Surely brave Mr Toad wouldn't mind coming here by himself, would he?" inquired the Mole.

"Old Toad?" said the Rat, laughing heartily. "He wouldn't show his face here for a hatful of guineas."

The Mole was cheered by the sound of the Rat's laughter, as well as by the sight of his stick and his gleaming pistols, and he stopped shivering and began to feel himself again.

"Now then," said the Rat, "we really must make a start for home. It will never do to spend the night here."

"Dear Ratty," said the poor Mole, "I'm simply dead beat. Let me rest a while longer, and get my strength back."

"O, all right," said the Rat. "It's nearly dark now, anyhow; and there ought to be a bit of a moon later."

So the Mole got well into the dry leaves and stretched out, and dropped off into sleep; while the Rat covered himself up for warmth, and lay waiting, with a pistol in his paw.

When at last the Mole woke refreshed and in his usual spirits, the Rat said, "I'll just see if everything's quiet."

He went to the entrance of their retreat and put his head out. Then the Mole heard him saying to himself, "Hullo! hullo! here – *is* – a – go!"

"What's up, Ratty?" asked the Mole.

"*Snow* is up," replied the Rat; "or *down*. It's snowing hard."

The Mole, looking out, saw the wood quite changed. Holes, pitfalls, and other black menaces were vanishing fast, and a gleaming carpet of faery was springing up everywhere.

"Well, it can't be helped," said the Rat. "We must make a start, I suppose. The worst of it is, I don't exactly know where we are. And this snow makes everything look so very different."

It did indeed. The Mole would not have known that it was the same wood. However, they set out bravely, and took the line that seemed most promising.

An hour or two later they pulled up, weary, and hopelessly at sea, and sat down on a fallen tree-trunk. They were aching, and bruised with tumbles; they had fallen into several holes and got wet through; the snow was getting so deep they could hardly drag their little legs through it. There seemed to be no end to this wood, and no beginning, and no difference in it, and, worst of all, no way out.

"We can't sit here," said the Rat. "We shall have to make another push for it. There's a sort of dell down there, where the ground seems all hilly and hummocky. We'll make our way down into that, and try and find some sort of shelter, and we'll have a rest before we try again. Besides, the snow may leave off, or something may turn up."

So they got on their feet, and struggled down into the dell, where they hunted about for a cave or corner that was a protection from the keen wind and the whirling snow, when suddenly the Mole tripped up and fell forward on his face with a squeal.

"O, my leg!" he cried. "O, my poor shin!" and he sat up on the snow and nursed his leg in both his front paws.

"Poor old Mole!" said the Rat kindly. "You don't seem to be having much luck today, do you?"

"I must have tripped over a hidden branch or a stump," said the Mole miserably. "O my! O my!"

"It's a very clean cut," said the Rat, examining it. "That was never done by a branch or a stump. Looks as if it was made by a sharp edge of something metal. Funny!"

"Well, never mind what done it," said the Mole, forgetting his grammar in his pain. "It hurts, whatever done it."

But the Rat, after tying up the leg with his handkerchief, was scraping in the snow.

Suddenly he cried "Hooray! Hooray-oo-ray-oo-ray-oo-ray!" and executed a feeble jig.

"What *have* you found, Ratty?" asked the Mole, hobbling up.

"A door-scraper! Why dance jigs round a door-scraper?"

"But don't you see what it *means*, you – you dull-witted animal?" cried the Rat impatiently.

"Of course I see what it means," replied the Mole. "It means that some *very* careless and forgetful person has left his door-scraper lying about in the middle of the Wild Wood, *just* where it's *sure* to trip *everybody* up!"

"O dear! O dear!" cried the Rat, in despair. "Here, stop arguing and come and scrape!"

After some further efforts, a very shabby door-mat lay exposed to view.

"What did I tell you?" exclaimed the Rat in great triumph.

"Nothing," replied the Mole, with perfect truthfulness. "You seem to have found another piece of domestic litter. Better dance your jig round that, and get it over, then perhaps we can go and not waste any more time over rubbish-heaps. Can we *eat* a door-mat? Or sleep under a door-mat? Or sit on a door-mat and sledge home on it?"

"Do – you – mean – to – say," cried the excited Rat, "that this door-mat doesn't *tell* you anything?"

"Really, Rat," said the Mole pettishly. "Who ever heard of a door-mat *telling* anyone anything? They simply don't do it. They are not that sort at all."

"Now look here, you – you thick-headed beast," replied the Rat, really angry, "this must stop. Not another word. Scrape, scratch and dig, if you want to sleep dry and warm tonight."

The Rat attacked a snow-bank, probing with his cudgel everywhere and digging with fury; and the Mole scraped busily too, more to oblige the Rat than for any other reason, for his opinion was that his friend was getting light-headed.

Some ten minutes' hard work, and the point of Rat's cudgel struck something hollow. He called the Mole to come and help him. Hard at it went the two animals, till at last in the side of what had seemed to be a snow-bank stood a solid-looking little door, painted a dark green. An iron bell-pull hung by the side, and below it, on a small brass plate neatly engraved in square capital letters, they read:

# MR BADGER

The Mole fell backwards on the snow from sheer surprise. "Rat!" he cried, "you're a wonder! A real wonder, that's what you are. I see it all now! You argued it out, step by step, in that wise head of yours, from the moment I fell and cut my shin, and you looked at the cut, and your majestic mind said, 'Door-scraper!' And then you found the door-scraper. Did you stop there? No. Some people would have been quite satisfied; but not you. 'Let me find a door-mat,' says you to yourself. And of course you found your door-mat. You're so clever, I believe you could find anything you liked. 'Now to find that door!' says you. Well, I've read about that sort of thing in books, but I've never come across it in real life. You're simply wasted here, among us fellows. If I only had your head, Ratty—"

"But as you haven't," interrupted the Rat rather unkindly, "I suppose you're going to sit on the snow all night and *talk*? Get up and hang on to that bell-pull, and ring as hard as you can, while I hammer!"

While the Rat attacked the door with his stick, the Mole sprang up at the bell-pull, clutched it and swung there, both feet well off the ground, and from quite a long way off they could faintly hear a deep-toned bell respond.